WAR STORIES
Of The U.S. Military
In
VIETNAM

Book Cover and Interior design by Alex P. Johnson

ISBN 13
978-1-63132-166-5

Library of Congree Control Number: 2022910280

Library of Congress Cataloging-in-Publication Data
is available upon request.

First Edition

Published in the United States of America by ALIVE Book Publishing
an imprint of Advanced Publishing LLC
3200 A Danville Blvd., Suite 204, Alamo, California 94507
alivebookpublishing.com

PRINTED IN THE UNITED STATES OF AMERICA

10 9 8 7 6 5 4 3 2 1

WAR STORIES
Of The U.S. Military
In
VIETNAM

Lt. William E. Freeman

ABOOKS
Alive Book Publishing

Lt. William E. Freeman

Contents

ONE

STORIES OF THE UNITED STATES MILITARY AT WAR

These stories are taken from the secret files of an organization, known as HU-R-ON, contracted to the Department of the Army. The files of HU-R-ON, Human Resource of Niagara, are closed.

After the Vietnam War the Army felt it had no use for jungle trained fighters. Like it had after every war, the United States Military downsized to prewar conditions and waited for the next war to come along.

It has been over 50 years since I revisited my diary, which I kept as a chronicle of my exploits along with a group of men who never really existed and were the bravest and most dedicated fighters of the war that was never declared. After the war these brave men had their contracts canceled and they returned to civilian life never to speak of their bravery and dedication. As such they were not eligible for the benefits due to the rest of America's fighting men and women. Their only reward was the knowledge that they contributed as much and more to the war effort as anyone who wore the uniform of the United States.

Even now, as I read my chronicles, my pride swells inside my chest and my heart beats faster. To finally write the exploits of the brave men who cannot exist even to this day, that I tell their stories of bravery and dedication. I must say that these stories are in truth an act of fiction.

It is because these men worked for the HU-R-ON organization that I called them Hurons and they never felt insulted. They took great pride in their heritage and being Americans.

My hope is that you read these stories and are entertained. They are taken from the fuzzy memory of an old 2nd. Lieutenant who was put out to pasture and probably should have stayed there.

JOIN US NOW AS WE PRESENT THE EXCITING STORIES OF "HURONS ON PATROL"

TWO

WAKING UP WITH
THOUGHTS FROM THE PAST

I woke up this morning thinking of my early years. It's my early years that made me what I became in my military service. I know it sounds strange, but I think my catharsis began last night. We are what we are because, in part, of what we were.

My story began because of my grandfather. I think I was around five years old when I became bi-racial. My Grandfather was a Cherokee Indian by birth, but he was a white man for most of his life. When I came along, he decided I should have the privilege of sharing his early life as an Indian. He packed my clothes, tossed them into the back of his pickup and deposited me at the front door of the Cherokee Nation in Oklahoma.

I was fair skinned and had white hair. I did not blend in. However, I tanned to a bronze color quickly. My hair was another story. I loved being steeped into the Indian culture. This is where I first found out that I was a half breed. Unloved by the Indian and hated by the white tribe. I learned about the Indian weapons and how to track. I also learned how to fight. I went to the Indian school for my school learning. That amounted to very little when I was thrust into white schools later in life. In all I enjoyed learning about my heritage and was able to blend it into what became my white life.

My parents moved to the San Francisco Bay Area when

I was nine. They took me with them. Four years of being an Indian and now I began to become white. We moved to the little town of El Sobrante, CA. A one room schoolhouse with first through fourth grades on one side of a partition and fifth and sixth on the other. Very rural and real country. Loved it. No desert! This is where I grew up. Here I wasn't a half breed. It's from here that I graduated from high school and hired out into railroad service. There I stayed until Uncle Sam decided my service was needed. I had no idea my early upbringing would be needed in a little country on the other side of the world.

I was drafted into the Army of the United States, three days before President Kennedy was shot. There I was at Fort Ord, CA wondering what was going to happen. That's where I learned that worrying wasn't going to change a thing so press on. While at Fort Ord, my distant past caught up with me. My Indian heritage singled me out. I was questioned about what I knew and how I had been brought up along with my early training. They seemed pleased and ordered me to Officer Candidate School. The school trained young officers to lead men and prepared us to fight a war in Europe. No mention was made about guerrilla warfare or jungle warfare. Nothing! I guess just being leaders of men was what was important. After graduation we were sent to Viet Nam. Not me! I was sent to a very secret place in Fort Benning, Georgia that I did not know existed.

Special Weapons Evaluation! Special Tactics Evaluation! What's going on? It was here that I was issued the first ten CAR-15 rifles. These were the collapsible stock models of the Armalite Rifle-16 (AR-16). And it was here that I received my tomahawk. Being taught how to fight with that is a story all its own.

I was loaded aboard a 707-jet airplane in Atlanta and flown into Viet Nam. I learned who I was supposed to be on the way over. We landed at night and a very large E-7 (Sergeant) picked me out of the crowd, loaded me and my gear along with a crate of special rifles and headed toward the unknown. Now, I was in the war.

THREE

HU-R-ON TO THE RESCUE

After graduating from Officers Candidate School (OCS) and becoming a newly minted 2nd Lieutenant, I was sent to a very secret unit located at Fort Benning, Georgia. My first duty posting was only about a mile from the OCS training. Unknown to me, I had been surveilled my entire time in the Army. Further training began immediately. Full blooded Indians began to further my education and field training taking me deeper into our indigenous people's way of life. My childhood really helped me to blend into and appreciate what was being taught. Enduring hunger and building muscle mass. Tracking was emphasized along with a basic understanding of the HU-R-ON language. What would I be doing to have a use of the HU-R-ON language? HU-R-ON it turns out is a private company that I would be working for. Their employees were Native Americans as such they were called Hurons.

HU-R-ON language it turns out is an amalgam of languages produced by computer so that their operatives can communicate with each other in secret. The use of the bow, and its special war arrows, and how to fight with a Tomahawk was phase two. I truly felt I had been transported back to colonial America. It was during this time that I was introduced to the Colt Automatic Rifle-15 (CAR-15). The carbine, collapsible stock version, of the Armalite Rifle-16

(AR-16). Hand to hand fighting with a Tomahawk while carrying the Army's new wonder weapon. I was issued ten of them and ordered to Vietnam. What could go wrong?

I had been with HU-R-ON for about a month learning how to put my knowledge of Indian tracking and modern weapons to work with the Huron ability to track and use their bows. I had arrived with Uncle Sam's latest generation of automatic rifle. The Hurons had been sent into combat with M-14 Springfield rifles. Although they had a selector switch which, when rotated, made the M-14 fully automatic. It also made that rifle a useless anti-aircraft weapon. No one could hold that rifle level and pointed toward the enemy after the first round went downrange. The muzzle of that rifle would rise up higher and higher and would force the rifle to the rear taking your hands with it. It was a wonderful rifle to fight yesterday's wars. The Army could have used it in World War II and especially the Korean War. That rifle along with the Korean War uniform was standard issue when I entered into the U.S. Army. We were trained to fight a European style war against the Russian Army. After all of that training, we were sent to Vietnam to fight a Guerrilla style war in the jungle. Most of our troops learned about the M-16 rifle while on the ships that transported them to Vietnam. That AR-16 was the Mk-1 version which had lots of teething problems.

Our small group trained and trained and then we trained some more. Finally. I thought we were ready for anything the powers to be could throw at us. And throw at us they did. We were assigned to rescue a small group of soldiers that had been separated from their main force. As they were just a few clicks (kilometers) away we decided to walk in to get them. Helicopters were great but not stealthy. We were very quiet. My men went into their Hooch and began their purification rituals. hot, steam enhanced with the smell of herbs. When they came out, they were covered with their signature war paint, stripped to the waist, and wearing vests covered with snaps and loops that they used to carry their war tools. They were also wearing their special steel mesh soled moccasins.

We assembled in front of the Hooch and checked our equipment. Each of them had a CAR-15 strapped to their back and carried a bow with Army-issued arrows. These were not standard arrows but arrows that came from a laboratory. They were real killers. This is where working for the CIA had merit. My radioman and I had standard issue. Off we went. We had the coordinates to where the men were supposed to be, but we knew that it was just a guess. Each of the men carried a Kukri knife along with a Tomahawk. The Kukri was used to cut a path through the jungle, the Tomahawk was used to cut a path through the human body. The Huron were serious fighters. We pushed through the jungle until night. It is too easy to lose your way at night, so I called a halt. We listened to the radio for the men we were seeking. We did not answer to any transmissions. The enemy had radios too. At first light we ate two energy bars along with a few sips of water and checked our coordinates and began our final push toward the men we were seeking. As we closed, we began to feel the presence of the enemy. It's a creepy feeling, but distinct. Our point man saw someone ahead of him wearing the wrong uniform and put an arrow in him. The man dropped where he stood, and we passed by him. Another two men ahead also took Huron arrows and dropped.

We began to fan out to cover as much ground as possible. Six more arrows and six men dropped. We moved closer. Ahead of us we could see what was left of the enemy. They did not have a clue as to how many of their troops were left. We noted that two of them were officers, so we took out the men they had left and took the officers prisoners. At this time, we recovered the arrows, we never left them behind.

The men we were sent to rescue were a sorry lot. They were hungry and scared witless when we surprised them. They thought that they were dead men when they saw the Hurons. I quickly explained that we were there to rescue them. As I gathered them together, I also made sure they knew we were in charge and that their ranks meant nothing to us. They were still scared when the Hurons started them on their way home.

That ended our first assignment. We dropped off the soldiers at their camp and proceeded home. The captives we hung on to and delivered to the CIA for interrogation. Apparently, those officers were high up the chain of command and knew many things the CIA wanted to know. I was proud of my men and told them so. They were uninterested with my thanks and wanted ice cream.

Not only did I procure all they could eat, but I also joined them in their feast. We were a happy and close-knit unit.

FOUR

INTERESTING TIMES

Way back; no, way, way back. Back when I had no idea what I would do in the Army. As a draftee, I had no idea what the Army did. I knew the Army protected the United States. I knew there were various branches that sounded interesting. I really wasn't interested in any of them. I had always thought of myself as a Navy man. Patrol boats, submarines, get in get out fast. Small units but essential to overall operations. One problem! This problem had been with me since age three. I'm deaf in my right ear. Can't tell which way sound comes from. So, I, along with everyone else, knew that I was immune from the draft and any service branch I might like to join. Wrong, Wrong, Wrong! Sounds like the bells I'm always hearing.

I got my draft notice at age 22. I went down to the Army pre-induction center and took the pre-induction physical. I failed three hearing tests. I went home knowing I had seen the last of my military life. My, my, how wrong can one guy get? My draft notice said Greetings from the President. The nation must have wanted me really bad for the President to personally invite me to the dance. What a dance it turned out to be. I went from a drafted Private to a Second Lieutenant in a few months. Little did I know how full my dance card would be.

I had specialized training with the use of a bow along

with specialized arrows. The shafts were made of tita-
nium. They were as light as a feather and tipped with a
stainless multi-pronged, what I was told to be, a Warhead.
It was awesome. Along with the bow I was trained to use
a close quarter instrument known as a Tomahawk. This
was a throwback to the early days of our country when the
indigenous Indian tribes fought each other and the Colonial Settlers.

With my training complete, I was told to report to the
Command Center of Fort Benning, Georgia where all of
my training had taken place. I was told I was assigned
through the Central Intelligence Agency (CIA) to the
Human Resource On Niagara department (HU-R-ON).
This was an experimental group contracted through the
Army. This group studied how to use native Indians in a
jungle environment. I was to be the liaison officer between
the Indian fighters and Central Command Vietnam. As I
was fitted out with all of the gear thought to be needed in
Vietnam, I was told that everything was to be considered
secret, need to know, and deniable. We did not exist. This
means that if anything went wrong, we would not be held
accountable to the Army. Although I was in charge of my
group, they actually worked for HU-R-ON. We called the
Indian fighters Hurons.

I was issued a .45 caliber Colt semi-automatic pistol.

A new type of jungle clothing.

Large brim foldable hat

Jungle boots containing wire mesh insoles.

One Tomahawk

And, last but not least, one crate containing ten CAR-
15 rifles.

The CAR-15 was a collapsible stock Armalite Rifle. This

rifle along with its Armalite Rifle16 (AR-16) counterpart was newly issued to the Army. CAR-15 and AR-16 does not mean Automatic Rifle. It means Armalite Rifle models 15 and 16. Armalite, was the original manufacturer of the rifle, but they could not build enough to supply an army. As such they sold the rifle to Colt Industries for manufacture.

So, there I was, being loaded aboard an aircraft in the middle of the night at Fort Benning airport. No one was there to give me a send-off. It was as if I did not exist.

FIVE

ON PATROL WITH HU-R-ONS

Indian Soldiers of the United States Military

This story is about my experience with Huron. HU-R-ON. Human Resource on Niagara. An experimental corporation that was using American Indians in the US ARMY. I called them all Hurons. I still wake up with chills after dreaming about what once was my duty. It's nothing I'm ashamed about, war is war and winning beats losing by a country mile.

I was assigned to a group that had no name and no history. I, along with my radio man, were the only white men in the group. We had no timetable. After each mission we stood down to let the water settle, so to speak. My group consisted of a small band of Indians from the upper east coast area. They had been recruited to reach out and get information and harass the enemy in a special way.

When we decided to take the fight to the enemy in our special way, no one in our area was alerted. We just disappeared into the jungle. My men would spend the afternoon in a sweat lodge breathing in a special combination of spirit gas to put them in the proper mood. While inside of the lodge they would strip down to bear chests and pants, put on their war paint and special steel mesh Moccasin footwear and Flak Vests. As evening approached, we would gather in front of their 'Medicine Hootch'. When I looked at these men, I shuttered thinking of the Colonial farmers who faced them with muzzle loading single shot Muskets. They were the most terrifying soldiers I had ever encountered. There they stood all painted up, carrying Gurkha knifes to cut their way through the jungle along with their Army issue Tomahawks. None had rifles. Only Recurved short Bows and Arrows. Just my Radio man and I had long arms. You had to see it to believe it. On my signal they moved out into the jungle making their own trail. Every 15 minutes they would stop and sample the air. None of them smoked or used smokeless tobacco. If nothing was detected, they would move out again. They moved so quietly and fast it was difficult to keep up. Rifles, ammo, and the radio are heavy.

One evening while on patrol they detected something. What they detected I did not know. They alerted and moved off to our right. They were spread out and moved very quietly and slowly. I followed about ten feet behind. There was a commotion ahead and when I got there, I found an enemy encampment along with several Viet Cong lying there dead. The men used their bows to silence the guards and finished the rest with the Tomahawks. I had never seen anything like it in my years of service. The jungle remained quiet as if nothing had happened. The men were searching the dead for papers and other military objects.

Suddenly one of the enemy who was not quite dead rose up and ran to me. I grabbed him and he held on to me. My Hurons wanted to take him, but I needed a live informant who would be glad to answer my questions rather than be thrown to them. He was a Major who knew quite a lot about troop strength and supply.

My Hurons wanted him dead. They did not believe in leaving survivors to talk about them. I assured them that he would be turned over to the CIA for questioning. The CIA was the group we worked for. That man clung on to me all the way back to camp. He wanted no part of those Hurons.

That Major was a lucky man. Hurons don't believe in prisoners. They feel that the dead can speak just as loudly and leave no evidence. When we returned to camp the Hurons returned to their "Medicine Hootch" for cleansing. They donned their regular Army issue fatigues and rejoined the world with no hint of their real role in the Army of the United States.

All of this story is still considered secret. Now that over 50 years have passed, I feel it's time to tell a few of the stories and experiences of a minor officer in the employ of the United States Army.

Now you know why I, as a member of a special force, was issued a Tomahawk.

SIX

SECRETS BEST LEFT UNTOLD

I was told to never mention my escapades in the Vietnamese jungles. As such I am telling my stories as if they were dreams made up as fantasies in the memories of an old man. It's like I was a congressman being questioned. I forgot! I don't remember! Could you be more specific? Did they really take place? No one really knows except me. No names will be mentioned because I've forgotten them. Dates? I've forgotten them also. Do we really want to know? Let's put it this way. They are as real as I can make them. So, let's just enjoy them as we dance around in the shadows.

It was early November 1965; we were on another mission of fact finding. Moving through the jungle and stopping periodically to listen as we always did. We were on our way to a village known to harbor the Viet Cong. At our last stop before surrounding the suspect village we heard pigs squealing and people yelling. We made note of the commotion and decided the village was under attack. My scouts moved closer and made visual contact. Members of the North Vietnamese Army (NVA) were burning the village and killing the livestock. They had gathered the population together and were questioning the males. We watched as they would kill one or two and begin questioning again.

We watched and formed a plan to rescue what was left

of the villagers. We figured silence was not an option, so we dropped the bows and untied our CAR-15s. My men moved to have a clear field of fire and proceeded to open fire at the NVA. The soldiers had no idea that there were any firearms in the village and panicked. They began to run into each other as they tried to get away. We, after the initial volley, began to pick them off one at a time. There was no stopping us as we eliminated the villager's oppressors. The Hurons faded back into the jungle and stood guard. My radioman, who was also our medic, and I, approached the people and began to give aid and what comfort we could.

I radioed to our base to send medical help to the coordinates of the village. I explained what had occurred, not mentioning our role in the matter, just that the village had been attacked by the NVA. We waited until the medical helicopters arrived then we retreated back to base. I heard the villagers had been frightened by strange looking devils who appeared and then disappeared after the fighting.

I would love to hear the stories told by the parents to their children of that village to make them behave. Some of them might have a bit of truth.

As the blues singer Fats Waller would say "One never knows do one"!

SEVEN

AXE ON PATROL

It has been over 50 years and I still get 'Night Sweats!' The throbbing of helicopter rotors, the pinging of incoming rounds passing through the thin skins of the Huey Helicopters. Over 50 years!

Once a young man of 25 and now a bent and used up old man of 80. I guess some memories are forever. I have been fighting a 22-foot-long python every night since the war.

My men and I were on a long-range patrol (LRP), deep in the jungles of Vietnam. I was about five men deep in a string of soldiers picking our way through dense foliage. Suddenly there was a very-large explosion off to our right shaking the ground. The men squatted down and waited; I was next to a large tree. There was a rustling of leaves overhead. I looked up and an exceptionally large and heavy python fell on top of me. The shock of the impact crushed me to the ground. Not being able to bring firearms into the equation, I reached for my tomahawk. This weapon was only issued to specialized forces and, as such, I had one. As the snake coiled itself around me my men were busy uncoiling it. I concentrated on the head. The head on that thing was as big as mine with fangs and teeth and a long-forked tongue. Spitting and hissing it stared into my eyes and I saw death. My tomahawk sliced into its long neck once, twice and with the third blow severed its head. The body thrashed around dragging me and my men with it. After several minutes the men were able to free me from the coils of the snake. We measured the body and found it to be 22-feet long. We could not find its head. After all that commotion I decided to end the Patrol and return to Basecamp. The legend of that snake and my Tomahawk grew by the week and did so until I rotated home.

Even now I keep that Tomahawk next to my bed just in case that head finds me.

EIGHT

GET COLONEL CHU'

S ounds simple, get Colonel Chu. The orders were delivered to us at the front gate of our compound. A dispatch rider, on a motorcycle, had arrived at our front gate. No one was allowed into our compound unescorted. Even the guards who were South Vietnamese were not allowed past the front gate. So, as usual, it was me carrying two cokes who answered the call. I signed for the orders and the driver rode off. I handed the cokes to the guards, which made them very happy, and I returned to our headquarters.

I called my HURONS to join me and proceeded to open 'the mail'. There inside the pouch were our latest orders. At the top in bold letters were two exceptionally large words Colonel Chu. Colonel Chu! The biggest, badest colonel in the North Vietnamese Army. He was in charge of the Prisoner of War camps. He would be the crown jewel in our efforts to exchange prisoners of war. He was worth many of our men. We were to risk everything we had to get him. No matter what it took we were to extract him from North Vietnam. I was standing while I read that to my men. Now I had to sit down. The excitement in the room was overwhelming. My guys were ready to go. I knew this would take careful planning, I had to get the helicopter pilots onboard which meant more people involved. Supplies meant more people. I needed as few personnel involved as possible. Secrecy was everything.

The plans told us of the colonel's itinerary. Which train he would be riding, where he would make his stops and how many troops would be with him. Mainly the route he would be taking was the most important. We had to figure how to separate him from his protectors. That was going to be the most dangerous part of our plan. We knew he had a very special passenger railcar that could be attached to the rear of any train going his way. The rear third of the car was very plush befitting a man of his importance. The forward two thirds held his bodyguards and supplies. All we needed was an ex-railroad man who was stupid enough to think he could take on the job of eliminating the soldiers and stopping the train at just the right time. I wondered who that might be. Of course, I thought, that would be me!

Flying along dangling from a rope just above a speeding train in the dark, what more could you ask for. Trying to signal the helicopter to lower me three more feet was really tough. I did not want to drop those few feet. Not only would I probably fall off the car, but the noise of my landing would alert anyone waiting inside. Down we went and I was able to release the rope and watch the helicopter fly away. Our plan was for me to stop the train as it entered a tunnel a few miles ahead. My men would be waiting on both sides of the track. I moved forward to the front of the car then climbed down its ladder to the platform. I attached a small explosive to the door handle and blew it away. I tossed a container of tear gas inside and climbed back on the roof and worked my way toward the rear. Looking down I saw two guards on the rear platform looking around wondering what was happening. I shot them and climbed down to the rear platform. Swinging out to look forward I saw the locomotive's headlight enter the tunnel. I then swung around and hanging on by one hand and standing on the rear step of the car I reached over the rear of the car next to the coupler for the airbrake handle, lifted it, turned it toward the rear, and waited for the rush of air escaping from the air hose to automatically set the emergency brakes.

Pulling myself back onto the platform I entered the rear of the car and confronted who was inside. The train came to a quick halt, and I was able to take control of the famous Colonel Chu. My men were in a fight with the guards who tried to exit the car. They did not put up much of a fight dazed and coughing from the teargas. I radioed one of the trailing helicopters to land and take the colonel. The remaining two helicopters were able to land and extract the rest of my men including myself.

Off we flew into the night hoping we had had enough excitement to last us for a long time. Once again, my past had caught up with me, proving that you should be careful in what you do in life because it just might come back to haunt you.

My crowning glory from this episode was my men finally accepting me as one of their own. I became a Blood Brother to the HURONS, not just the officer in charge.

NINE

QUICK ON THE DRAW

We were returning from a mission at the front edge of our territorial boundaries. It always sounded strange to me that there were limits a unit could not exceed in a time of war. Limits can really put a strain on your ability to pursue an enemy. So, of course, we never crossed that fine line. I can feel my nose growing already.

We received over our radio instructions for me to report to our field headquarters as soon as possible. We had been returning by helicopter, very unusual for us, and now I was about to find out why. Not wanting to look like something the cat dragged in, I took the time to clean up and get a Jeep ride to headquarters. There they were wearing suits, our bosses. My thoughts were impure. Nothing but trouble. Even I was amazed when they began to tell me about the mission they had in mind. A peace keeping mission. Seems two of our allied tribes were having a territorial dispute. The two tribes were made known to me and I cringed. These guys were Headhunters. There was no way a mere 2nd Lieutenant was going to make them do anything. The suits informed me that they knew that I was known to raise myself in rank when the need arose. I told them that these guys only did business with Colonels and above. They agreed and proceeded to give me all the needed badges of rank and a highly polished helmet liner, shiny black, with a full Colonels eagle attached to it. I was impressed. We were to use both squads of Hurons, including the second squads Lieutenant, now dressed as a Captain. We had full, oral, permission to deal with the situation as needed.

We returned to our base and proceeded to tell our men about the mission. Not one of them volunteered to go on this seemingly impossible mission. I had asked for volunteers, but I knew they would go anyway. My number two in command decided I needed to look the part of a bad ass field Colonel, so they proceed to spit shine my jump boots. Pulled out my Khaki dress uniform. Khaki is an obsolete tan uniform more associated with World War II and on its way-out during Vietnam. But it would be perfect now. The men put all kinds of medals on the shirt. And then the crowning glory to this uniform was my chrome plated, fully engraved, Ivory-handled Colt .45 single action, six-gun with holster. A going away present from my fiancé. I looked just like General. George Patten. I liked what I saw.

We began loading our third helicopter with trade goods. We knew they would be highly prized by the tribes. The other two helicopters were for us. Each squad had their own. Fully loaded we lifted off and proceeded toward the mountains. The mountain area was mainly devoid of trees, so we had no problem landing. I had the other two helicopters land first to deploy the men, my personal guard. I then had my helicopter hover 3-feet off the ground to create a swirling dirt and dust cloud before landing. I emerged through the cloud of dust like Gen. MacArthur returning to the Philippines. Everyone was impressed. I, taking long strides, approached the tribal leaders. There I stood looking down on them, through my sunglasses and asked what the problem was. They began to speak to me simultaneously. I held up my hand and they stopped. I told them the first thing I was going to do was pass out gifts. I had my men off load the helicopter and spread the items out on the grown. I had the chiefs pass through the items to pick what they wanted. Then I had the people of the villages go through and find what they wanted. Everyone was happy. A good way to begin negotiations.

We were taken to a small hut that had been built in the middle of the village. We entered, my assistant, the captain entered first followed by the tribal leaders and then I entered. We were seated on folding chairs and began our talks. Everything was very pleasant, and I could not understand why we were needed. Then the reason for the turmoil entered. He was a very large vicious looking individual. He had an AK-47 strapped to his body. He wanted to take over both villages and was going to kill anyone who interfered. The people of the villages did not know what to do. He was yelling and boasting about his strength and willingness to kill anyone. He came over to me and put his ugly face next to mine and challenged me to a fight. I stood up looked him in the eye and agreed. We would meet in the middle of the village where the negotiation hut had stood. He boasted that he would put many holes in me with his AK. So, there we stood looking at each other 50 feet apart. He was holding his rifle across his chest as we waited for a signal from the Leaders to shoot. As the hands went up, I drew and fired. I shot him dead center of mass. He fell over backward and did not twitch. I was not about to have a fair shooting match with that guy.

Everything calmed down. The village elders became

friends again, which was good for us, as they kept track of the North Vietnam Army (NVA). We packed up leaving one dead. This duel, which was agreed upon by all parties, could not be classified as a murder. Which was good for me. The United States soldiers were often given Article 15s, for supposed infractions against what they perceived as enemy combatants. Being a soldier can have a heavy burden.

We returned to base with our mission accomplished. Everyone was happy. I called my fiancé and told her how useful her going away present was. She laughed and said she would send the matching Colt .45 right away. Now there is a woman who looks after her man. All of the years of belonging to an association of 'Cowboy Fast Draw' really paid off. I am renewing my membership this payday.

THE MORAL TO THIS STORY IS SHOOT FIRST- ASK QUESTIONS LATER!

TEN

A GREAT WEAPON

I never thought of a handheld radio being used as a weapon of war. Yes, I know that a walkie talkie is used during action in a combat situation. Thusly it is a weapon of war. But in almost all cases it is just a communications device. Sometimes, I repeat sometimes, it works as such.

We were on one of our many patrols of which we already know they are out there; we already know who we are after and generally we know how many we will be bringing back. We were weeding the garden, so to speak. They were on alert as is everyone who ventures into the Jungle. Their problem was that they were not expecting us. Using coordinates given to us before we left Basecamp we arrived before the North Vietnamese Army (NVA). We looked around and saw what was going to be their headquarters. It had been prepared for their arrival by North Vietnamese Engineers. We were impressed. I thought what a shame we were going to destroy it, as I thought we could make use of it ourselves.

We had brought along two large bags of electrical mines. These mines could be exploded by radio signal. Mines are explosive devices that are usually buried in roads and detonated by pressure of heavy vehicles rolling across them. But there are several uses of mines, and they are built for use in differing conditions. Ours were small anti personal remotely exploded devices. Perfect for what we wanted to do. What we wanted to do was control the battlefield. We carefully planted the mines in the sleeping quarters and around the Mess, eating area. We even put them in the toilets. One thing we did not do was place them anywhere we thought the Officers would be. We wanted the Steak not the Potatoes. We cut the jungle back to afford us clear fields of fire. They couldn't see us, but we could see them. We waited.

It was getting dark when the Scouts, everyone uses Scouts to clear the area from enemy combatants, came into the compound. They looked around and signaled the main group of soldiers to come on in. We waited and watched to see who were in charge. Almost all of the soldiers were in before the Officers made their entrance. We wanted everyone to be comfortable and relaxed. We watched as the soldiers went into the barracks to store their gear and watched as others went into the toilets. We saw the Officers gather together and started to talk among themselves.

The Officers were close together and away from their troops. We began to explode the mines in in the Barracks and then the Toilets were next to explode followed by the Mess area. We began to shoot as many of the soldiers that came out of the Barracks and Toilets as we could and began our assault on the Officers. The Officers were stunned and gave little resistance as we corralled them and shoved rifles into their faces. We began to extract ourselves and began to force our captives into the jungle. My radioman stayed with the rear guard to keep me informed as to what was going on. He was carrying a Walkie Talkie, a handheld two-way radio. He saw an NVA soldier take aim with his AK-47 at one of the rear guards and as the radio was in his hand, he threw it at him. The radio hit the soldier in the head, knocking him out. My radioman was now out of radio communication and headed for the Jungle with the rear guards. Our rear guards continued to shoot into the compound to discourage anyone from being a hero.

We retreated following the same trail we had made going in. Our rear guard covered the trail with the tree limbs we had cut to disguise our escape. My Hurons explained what would happen to the North Vietnamese Officers if they did not comply. They got the message and went along willingly. After two clicks, kilometers, almost two miles, we called a halt near a clearing we had found on the way in and called for a helicopter extract. The Pilots had us shine our flashlights in a large circle so that they could land. The helicopters had already been aloft when the call come in and as such took very little time to reach us. As we lifted-off we looked back toward the compound and saw the fires burning brightly in the Sunset. It's always a comfort to lean against the helicopters interior and feel that powerful engine carrying me home.

We got quite a pleasant surprise when we found out who these Officers were. They were part of an advance group who were sent to build a large forward base for the North Vietnamese Army so that the Army would have a base for operations in a coming attack on Saigon. Apparently, we were the main reason the attack was called off. All I can say is that no attack on Saigon was perpetrated while my Hurons were active around the area.

If you want to stop an attack call HU-R-ON

ELEVEN

ANOTHER WAY TO DIE IN VIETNAM

I was tossing and flaying about a couple of weeks ago while trying to sleep. The nightmares just won't go away. One in particular stands out from the crowd. Flying death. The image of those giant birds still gave me the shakes. Tiger Eagles! Believe me you have not been scared until you have to deal with eagles as big as California Condors. A wingspan of 9 feet and talons the size of a grown man hands.

Tiger Eagles live in the mountains above Cambodia, Thailand and Vietnam. They are rare and elusive. Seldom seen, but when they are it's usually too late for its prey. We found out about the birds, mainly from rumors, told by the highland tribes. The birds were spoken of in whispers along with furtive looks toward the sky. We had not heard of the birds and as such only thought of them as rumors and stories told to children to make them behave. Eagles were nothing to fear. Exaggerations were part of village life. We knew we could manage anything that could fly.

We were up in the highlands just skirting the edge of the jungle on the lookout for the North Vietnamese Army (NVA). We had been told that they were using this area to stage raids into the jungle then retreat back on to the highlands and disappear into the valleys of the mountains.

We had patrolled the area for days waiting and

listening to no avail. We stopped and made use of cover provided by a small stand of trees. It looked like an oasis standing there all by itself among the barren landscape. We were tired and cold from the altitude. We began to settle down and spread our gear. The limbs of the trees were swaying back and forth which we thought was caused by the light breeze that was making us cold. We relaxed.

Suddenly crashing down through the limbs and leaves were two giant birds. Screaming and slashing with their talons and beaks. Tiger Eagles were among us! We had never come across such violence. Those birds knew no fear and continued their attack. My men tried to bring their Tomahawks up for defense, but they were ripped out of their hands. There seemed to be no defense. The beaks and claws were tearing into the flesh of my men and blood was everywhere. My radioman was using his PRC 25 radio to ward off the strikes from the talons when the huge talons ripped the microphone cord away from the set which caused the radio to emit a high-pitched scream. The scream was much louder than those coming from the birds. It was that noise coming from the radio that caused the birds to stop their attack and fly off. We watched the birds circle overhead and worried that if they came back, we might not survive a second attack. Never again would I belittle tribal lore. They obviously knew far more than I would ever know about their history. I became a believer!

We laid down totally spent. Blood and torn clothing were everywhere. We began to bandage the most severely wounded. I took stock of our condition which was dismal. Fortunately, our radio man was an absolute genius with radio equipment and had our radio repaired in half an hour. We were in no condition to continue operations.

For the first time in my career, I had to call for a Medivac. I was exhausted. Give me full contact with the enemy anytime. I can manage that. But fighting birds? Humiliated and defeated, I cannot believe it to this day. What can I say to the powers that be? Who will believe it? I did get souvenirs. Several feathers that were larger than my hand. We are going to put one of them into our hats as a reminder to remember that we are not the apex killers walking this land. I called for four helicopters. No one will be walking home this time.

Never again would I consider myself superior toward a people we thought of as primitive.

TWELVE

NEVER A DULL MOMENT

Have you ever tried flying home after a busy day in the field? I have! My Huey pilot offered to give me lessons flying a helicopter. What joy! I never would have asked. Ground pounders aren't supposed to fly co-pilot. We already have a co-pilot. One who knows what he is doing but, when you are in a small independent group, such as ours, who's to know?

So, there I was flying everywhere but straight and level. After a few minutes, someone on the ground began to shoot at us. Our door gunner began to shoot back. I would never ever have the nerve he demonstrated by hanging out of that Huey. The only thing keeping him with us was a strap of webbing, attached to him and the M-60 machine gun. It looked like he had leveled every square inch of the jungle canopy below us. Unfortunately for us, the Huey's engine had taken a few rounds and was coming apart. The pilot calmly took the controls and headed for a small river that was, as we found, quite shallow. Down we went and landed with a splash. Our second helicopter, which contained the rest of my men landed alongside. The only damage was to our Huey. I decided that my men, along with myself would go on alone. The Huey crews would fly off and come back for us if needed. We helped load the M-60 machine gun into the other Huey then pulled back and watched them lift off and fly away. I can't say we were alone but what supplies we had was all we had. Being alone was what we did. In a way it was business as usual.

We were near a mountain I recognized, having flown over it a few times, and we had taken a compass bearing before landing. I was confident we could make it home without too much drama. I am reminded what the Army says is the most dangerous thing in the world would be a Second Lieutenant with a map and a compass. With those encouraging words running through my brain, I sent out my scouts and we began our trip home. Scouts are used to make sure the road or trail ahead is clear.

Humid and hot, a typical day in the jungle. We marched alongside of a small road that seemed too good to be true, When I say alongside of the road, I mean six feet from the road through the Jungle. On the road we could be ambushed or blown up by a mine. Only green G.I.'s walk down roads. I was really glad I had the men top off their canteens along with Iodine tablets, while standing in the river. Iodine kills bacteria enabling us to drink and not get sick. I began to see what I thought were tire tracks. I started to think that the road, in reality, was a supply road as I could see rice that looked as it was spilling out of something. Now I was nervous. What were we walking into? The only sounds we heard were from the monkeys and the tigers. Suddenly the column stopped. Word was passed back from the scouts that there was activity ahead. I went forward and observed an American Jeep with a trailer-in-tow stopped in the middle of the road. The trailer was loaded with bags from which rice was falling. Two North Vietnamese Army (NVA) soldiers were standing together alongside of the Jeep smoking and tying up rice bags. I knew right then the trail was not mined and that we could use it if a retreat was called for. We stood alongside of the men and listened to them talk. They were incredibly open with their conversation about their living conditions and how many men were in their company and how far they still had to go.

The NVA soldiers said it was five clicks, kilometers, to their compound. I felt we could pace-off four clicks and reenter the jungle. My men thought I was nuts but agreed to my plan. We waited for the soldiers to leave then off we went, half of the men on each side of the road. My scouts were 200-feet ahead. We were soaked with sweat, and it felt wonderful to be out of the Jungle. Our pace increased and what little breeze there was began to dry our uniforms. In about an hour we melted back into the jungle. Within 20 minutes we had contact. What was amazing was the lack of guards. No guards? Were they expecting us? We backed deeper into the jungle and began to circle the camp. What we found was a company having dinner. A heavy equipment company, they had large trucks and Jeeps with trailers, but what they had that held my interest were four 155mm howitzers. Siege guns! What were they meant for? All of this equipment was American. Our Headquarters needs to know this. But we could not use our radio. The NVA has our radios also. I needed to make a plan.

Everyone of my men carried one Thermite grenade. One never knows when one needs to weld something. We mapped out the area and found a truck that would hold all of us. Then we waited until dark. I carried two Thermite grenades and my scouts had two. Two grenades per cannon. The grenades would roll down the barrels and proceed to ignite and weld the breach closed. The breach is the end of a cannon that opens so you can shove a cannon shell inside and fire it.

We had found a truck along the edge of the company area that was also near the road out of the camp. The same road we followed to get to the camp. We had noted that the road seemed to run towards our planned exit. Dawn was approaching when we began running to the cannons and tossed the grenades inside. Thermite grenades do not explode like a regular grenade, they bubble and fizz and spark. But they do have a bright light.

There the cannons were, looking like beacons to the stars. We sprinted to the truck and as we exited the camp, we began to shoot up every vehicle within range. The whole camp looked like a bonfire. We could hear the explosions a mile away. There is nothing like a new truck with a full tank of gas. It was time to use the radio.

Our pilots were listening for our call. We told them of our situation and that a column of trucks should be hot on our trail. They responded that they were on the way and would be bringing company. I do not think that there is anything more beautiful than two Huey's coming to your rescue followed by four Huey Cobra Gunships. Our Huey's landed and the Gunships flew out of sight. As we loaded aboard, we could hear the sound of cannon and 30-caliber machine guns. Telling headquarters about our find might be a waste of time. I left two of my men to drive the truck to our base of operations. One never knows when one might need a truck.

I was ordered to Headquarters, never a good sign. Someone at the top wanted to know where all of that equipment came from. Since none of it was for sale to our allies something was amiss. We were to infiltrate North

Vietnam, by parachute, penetrate NVA Headquarters and find out where that equipment came from. Now I don't know about you, but that sounds like a death sentence to me. Maps and call signs were distributed, and a jump date was set for two weeks.

I returned to our compound and called everyone to the large hooch and began to tell my tale of woe. We would use both teams. One team in full HU-R-ON dress would make the penetration while the other team in regulation dress would provide security. The NVA headquarters was situated 30 miles inside North Vietnam. The Air Force would provide a C-47 to use as our jump plane, an aircraft in use since WWII the Air Force would bomb an area three-miles in diameter around the NVA headquarters and then move forward and bomb another three-mile section as we were landing for a diversion. We would spend the next two weeks practicing our jump techniques and attacking a building some 20 miles away from our compound. At this time, we were introduced to a Vietnamese General who would know what to look for in the files. Two weeks is a very short time to learn so much. The final briefing contained information gained from our spies. Like all information centers the action is taking place miles away so personnel are sparse at ground zero. That sounded excellent.

We gathered for the last time at the air base. We would be doing this at night so everything around us was blacked out. We took off at 2300 hrs. (11:00 pm). The flight was to take two hours and we were to land around 0100 hrs. As we approached, we could hear the bombs exploding ahead of us. The crew chief had us stand up, hook up and shuffle toward the door. The jump light changed from red to green and out we went. The night sky was ablaze from exploding bombs and tracers. We looked like a string of pearls dropping toward the ground. Landing was uneventful. We took stock of ourselves and headed for the Headquarters building. We only saw a few people outside of the building looking at the sky which our arrows took care of. As we approached the building our rear guard surrounded it and we entered. Upon entering the building, a lot of screaming took place as the people inside saw the HURONs approaching, again a few arrows quieted the rooms. We entered the records room and our general moved forward to examine the files. As I always say I like live high-ranking personnel, so my men searched for some. And what did they find? Two live, terrified out of their minds, colonels. They were talking so fast no one could understand them. So, we tied them up, taped their mouths and shoved them out the door.

Our general seemed satisfied with what he found so we signaled our rescue helicopters to land and pick us up. Away we went as if no one had been there. That is, if you don't count the fires, bodies and collapsed buildings. Our escort was two Huey Cobra Gunships. We had no worries.

And what did all of this give us? Seems like a very large and profitable black market was being run out of Saigon. Two generals, five full colonels, several high-ranking enlisted men, all American, along with assorted high-ranking Vietnamese.

My, my, what one will do to get an ill-gotten buck. Even betray the good old USA.

THIRTEEN
HUNG OUT TO DRY

I came to while being transported through the jungle on a litter, tied up and groggy. I wasn't sure, but I had good reason to believe I had been snatched from my compound while I made my rounds and talking to our Vietnamese guards. These guards are only used for guarding the main gate. They are not allowed inside the compound. The reason for that was made abundantly clear as I was being transported. I could feel the top of my head bleeding with the blood dripping down my face.

I knew they wanted me for information. I also knew that they would not have me long enough to torture and question me. I knew that my HURONS would be on their trail as soon as they realized I was not where I was supposed to be. I had not been gone 15 minutes before my guys were exploring the compound and perimeter for signs of where I had gone. Once found they were on their way. They found the bodies of four of the guards. One was missing. They quickly figured the fifth guard who had me was the leader of the Viet Cong (VC). They pressed on through the jungle stopping every 15 minutes to assay the situation. They were able to see drops of my blood as an indicator that I was still alive.

My captors reached a small clearing which they had made into a base camp. They rested and prepared food. They had no intention of staying long. They just needed enough time to boil water to cook some rice and get their wind back. They were really nervous and totally alert. Unknown to them the HURONS had made up the time and were listening to them as they talked in whispers, planning their next move. They moved quickly putting out the fire and removing any trace that they had been there. As they moved toward me, I saw two of them fall with arrows in their backs. The HURON war cry sent chills up my spine and I watched as every VC soldier went down with HURON arrows embedded in them. There was only one survivor. He was the guard, still in his uniform, who was guarding the gate when my abduction occurred. He was shaking and whimpering knowing what was going to happen to him upon our return to base.

The HURONS rebuilt the fire but made it far larger. When it was roaring, they began to drag the dead and tossed them onto it. My guys wanted to leave a warning as what will happen should this occur again. When we were ready to move out, I asked them to bandage my head to stop the blood flow. They just laughed and tossed a small bottle of iodine to me and told me to self-medicate. As we moved out, they told me I owed them big time. I already knew that, and I tried to figure out what I could get them out of my meager pay.

Maybe I'll get them some ice cream.

FOURTEEN

WAY OUT OF OUR WHEELHOUSE

There are times when others want to play in your sandpile. Times when those in charge want to show off and agree to things far beyond their mission statement. Just because the regular Army, governed from the Pentagon, wants to make sweeping moves on a map doesn't mean it will work in the field.

Case in point. The thought was that if they sent one 100 men to do battle with what they perceived to be inferior enemy soldiers, we would win and wind down the war and be home by Christmas. Home by Christmas did not work in a World War. WW1, which was called the 'Great War', until the Second World War came along, and we had to redo the math. For some reason, wars always have to be over by Christmas. Didn't work way back then and doesn't work today. Underestimation, I believe, is taught in war colleges around the world. They are not us; therefore, they cannot compete. Why? They are not us! We have the equipment; we have the best Air Force, and we have God on our righteous side. Therefore, we can blunder into undeclared war after war. So, what if we lose? Those in charge will never be held accountable. Wouldn't look good. As such we press on as if no one is to blame. Just bad luck. Could happen to anyone.

Now what does this have to do with us? They came knocking on our door because nothing went right. We, all

20 of us, are to be used to rescue what is left of a large body of men, who in effect, no longer resemble a fighting force. Our HU-R-ON group consisted of two squads of ten men. Each had eight fighters one Radioman/Medic and one Officer. The Army can afford to sacrifice a body of men who don't exist anyway to save reputations of generals who do exist. What could go wrong?

First thing to do is arrange for an Air Force to be assigned to us. This is to include six Huey Cobra Gunships. The Air Force had to assign several "Jolly Green Giant" HH-3E Helicopters, these are huge and hold many people. They are used to rescue pilots who have been shot down. Troop carrying Chinook CH-47 helicopters to move most of the soldiers out of harm's way. Assembling this many aircraft takes time. We used the time to find out where the troops were, what color smoke to be used. Smoke grenades are used to identify soldiers and tell others where the troops are. Radios need to be set to certain frequencies and hope the enemy is not listening to the same frequencies.

It took 12 hours to get my Air Force assigned and coordinated to begin the rescue. Each transport helicopter had a Medic onboard. I thought we were ready, and my Huey took off followed by the rescue force. I went ahead along with the Cobra Gunships to locate our soldiers. We followed the coordinates given by the soldiers on the ground. As we approached, I had the ground troops pop yellow smoke. This gave me an ariel view of the perimeter of the area the troops were in. I told them to hug the ground and sent the Gunships in to neutralize the surrounding area out to 100 yards.

The evacuation helicopters were stationed just short of

a mile behind us. As I circled, I had the commanding officers come out of the tree line so I could land near them.

After I unloaded supplies out of the Huey's door, I had
the helicopter fly back toward the Landing Zone (L Z) and
begin to drop off my men every 200 feet to form a line so
that the men evacuating could see which way to go. I had
the Huey Helicopters fly forward to pick up the wounded.
The Cobra Gunships began to neutralize the area out to
200 yards.

When I landed, we off loaded several crates of canteens
of cold water and four crates of 30 round, guaranteed to
work, magazines. These I gave to able bodied soldiers. I
gave them a canteen and two magazines and sent them to
form a line 30 yards away from the helicopters. I had six
Huey's loading and evacuating wounded and six Huey's
on the way to take the place of the loaded Huey's. I had
the officers whose men we were rescuing take charge and
I went to see how the loading of the large helicopters was
going.

I gathered my men, as they were no longer needed in
the line. As I approached the helicopter landing zone (L
Z), I could hear firing beyond the helicopters. My men
were engaged in a fire fight and we joined them. I sent five
of my men into the tree line to come up behind whoever
was firing at us. We tried to keep up a steady flow of bul-
lets to keep them low to the ground while my flanking
force delt with them. We heard a large volume of firing
coming from the tree line ahead and then all was quiet. I
left my men where they were for protection of the helicopters. I radioed the incoming helicopters to make sure they
weren't too close to the ascending aircraft and sent the
loaded helicopters on their way. This little plot of land was

just 100 yards long and was acting like an airport. It's amazing what can be done when forced to.

It took a total of four hours to evacuate everyone. I lost count of how many were wounded and or dead. I know one thing, no one was left behind. When everyone had been evacuated, I had the Huey Cobras shoot up the battle ground just in case there were any enemy souvenir hunters picking through the debris.

So ended another HU-R-ON story. A story to be filed away and added to the Chronicles. Stories of a small band of men of what the military now calls Contractors.

And now for the reason we were chosen to have the responsibility to affect a fighting evacuation and end the fiasco generated by Army Command. If we failed, the blame for the entire operation would fall on our shoulders. Army Command would be held blameless. It would be the Contractors who were at fault. If we pulled it off, Army Command would get the credit for a successful operation.

There is some good news that came from all of this. Two Full Colonels were promoted to Generals. The Two-Star General who dreamed up the idea was promoted to Three Stars.

I understand our invitation to the promotion party was lost in the mail.

FIFTEEN

FIGHTING FROM THE SKY

Who ever thought that Airborne soldiers, wearing war paint, dropping down from the sky would exist in the modern age of warfare. Not since D-day have soldiers of the United States painted themselves in warpaint to engage other soldiers. A soldier wearing war paint is a soldier who means business. Death from above would bring fear to anyone looking up and seeing Hurons descending upon them. Running would seem to be the best answer. Huron arrows bring a quiet death to those who choose that option.

We had gotten word that the North Vietnamese Army (NVA), had brought in mercenary soldiers from Burma, now Myanmar, to hunt down and kill the scourge of Hurons that infested the battlefield in Vietnam. Unfortunately for them HU-R-ON corporation had intercepted their communications and had laid plans to eliminate the mercenary force upon their arrival. Through a system of satellite observation, the mercenaries were tracked from their base in Burma through North Vietnam to a base in South Vietnam. HU-R-ON knew that the Burmese troops would be coming in three groups. Each group would be one day apart not wanting the confusion that would ensue if they arrived at the same time. A wonderful idea as far as logistics was concerned but a bad idea when the Hurons knew when they would arrive and at what time.

HU-R-ON Corp. notified the South Vietnamese about the plans of the Burmese and coordinated the Huron fighters along with two companies of South Vietnamese Army soldiers to arrange a surprise party for the Burmese soldiers. The South Vietnamese would surround the staging area letting the few trucks through and closing off their retreat. The airborne Huron fighters would ensure panic as they fell from the sky using automatic weapons and killing those directly below them with arrows. The South Vietnamese would eliminate the rest as they ran into the surrounding soldiers. As each group of Burmese would be a day apart this allowed a cleanup of the area, not wanting the Burmese to get suspicious as they drove into the staging area. We cleared a circular path for the trucks to follow and installed lights to light up the landing field. A generator was placed a distance away so it could not be heard over the truck noise. As the Hurons descended, the landing site would be bathed in light allowing the Hurons to do the maximum damage and land safely.

Just three-short vicious battles and the Burmese would just be a footnote in the Vietnamese war. Panic is a horrible condition when fighting. The Huron fighters spread the panic far and wide as they descended into the panicking mass of Burmese soldiers. Screaming their war cry, the Hurons fired their CAR-15s into the middle of the mass of enemy soldiers. Those that looked up were killed with the war arrows of Huron fighters. As the Hurons landed, they found only dead Burmese soldiers, the living had runoff into the rifles of the South Vietnamese soldiers who showed no mercy to the foreign mercenaries.

The cleanup took several hours, leaving the soldiers of the South just a few hours to rest and eat to renew their fighting strength. The Hurons were helicoptered to the air-field to rest and get aboard the airplane that would take them back into battle. A total of three times the Hurons parachuted into the night sky bringing panic and death. I was not invited to the Burmese going away party, as my men would say, I would have just been in the way. Where was I while the fun was taking place? I was back at Base listening to the radio and biting my fingernails. We had three men injured, mainly from landing on those Burmese fighters.

We all wondered what the North would dream up next to rid themselves of the dreaded Hurons. We reveled in the fact that they were staying up late at night trying to figure out where we would strike next.

Where would the Hurons strike next? It's a puzzle-ment, isn't it?

SIXTEEN

ORDERS FROM THE TOP

In November 1965, we received orders by courier. Normally our orders came to us by radio. We had several codes to keep transmissions secret. Something big was blowing in the wind. Now, after 50 years I can speak of it. This was a mission of the highest order.

Normally, we only dispatch a few of our fighters at a time. This mission called for everyone. We only had 20 combat soldiers, two Lieutenants and two radio operators. To involve everyone meant we had no reserve. We always had the comfort of knowing we had backup ready to go if we needed help. And now, no backup! We had a full Colonel in overall charge who could cancel any mission. He remained silent. No one could remember any orders coming by courier. We donned our full army combat gear and prepared to board two helicopters.

We told the men what the mission was about during the flight. Command had intercepted a message sent to the North Vietnamese Army, known locally as the NVA. The message reported to the troops in the field that a high-ranking general was coming for an inspection near Quang Tri Province. Generally, we worked out of an area near Hue. We were to refuel halfway and proceed to Quang Tri after dark. Landing helicopters in the dark worried me more than the combat missions we were sent on. Fortunately, there were Army Pathfinders who had been sent ahead to light the landing zone. We had four helos with us. Two continued on to divert the enemy troops. The Scouts also brought gasoline and began filling the helicopters as we left for our mission.

There's not a lot of cover to hide in near the coast. We used the grass and whatever vegetation we could secure to cover our bodies and moved out. Our men could move at a slow trot and would cover many miles without being fatigued. We had maps of the area and knew where the general would be during the evening hours. Our groups separated and began to surround the building where the general was sleeping. We didn't have the bows, but, as always, we had the Tomahawks. The HURONS were incredibly silent as they worked their way to the general's quarters. Three guards were overcome, and the general was trussed up and silenced and we began to make our exit. Four more guards fell to the Tomahawks, and we were off. The general was hung between two poles we had brought with us and, unknown to him, we had brought his uniform with us. We wanted him to look good while being interrogated.

After an hour we once again boarded our helicopters and 'bugged out'. As I understand it the general was very helpful. Many plans were changed because of his information. And yes, he looked good during interrogation. As for us, once again, we were told that nothing would be made of our efforts.

No medals, but I, of course, supplied everyone with their favorite ice cream.

SEVENTEEN

STEPPING OUT IN THE JUNGLE

How often have you taken a stroll in the jungle? That is what we did almost every day. Yeah, we did the *jungle trail two-step* almost daily. I am certain that you are asking what in the world is the *jungle trail two-step?* What indeed! Let me educate you about a lesser-known part of the jungle known as a Spider Hole. It's a well concealed hole in the jungle floor just off the beaten path. One comes across them quite by accident. But then again not quite by accident. Those are what we earned our pay finding.

These holes are entrances to underground tunnels. Tunnels that can lead to large dug-out areas being used by "Charlie". Now we all know who "Charlie" is. Charlie is the Viet Cong and/or South Vietnamese insurgents. They are the bad guys. Our opposition. They don't like us. We, on the other hand, think they misunderstood our intentions. Our intentions were to pave over that hellhole and use it for a parking lot.

Our group, quite small as infantry units go, seek out these tunnels. One usually finds them by stepping into one causing you to stumble and improvise a dance step. After clearing a perimeter around the hole, we prepare to enter it. Believe me it is dark and scary. Dangerous with a Capital D. Now you would think because it is so scary, we would send the biggest hairy-chested bar brawler down to kick and re-educate Charlie. No, no, that is not what happens. We pick the skinniest, shortest Hero we can find. Those tunnels are tiny. We give him a flashlight, a knife, and a .45 semi-automatic pistol. Even with all of that gear the most important thing he gets is cotton plugs for his ears. Most of the time he will not encounter anything, as Charlie will be "long gone." But sometimes he leaves us a present. Bamboo Pit Vipers, snakes tied to a stake, spiders by the dozen, again guaranteed to kill you. Worst of all are the miniature Punji-Sticks hidden in the floor of the tunnel smeared with human feces. And last but not least there is always the chance of meeting "Charlie" coming through the tunnel your way. That's what the ear plugs were for. A gunfight in a tunnel brings very loud noises. He who shoots first shoots last. At the sound of gunfire, we automatically pull him out. Hopefully no one comes out with him. It's for sure he'll be using the helicopter Medivac services. Lots of Purple Hearts were awarded to these brave soldiers.

If ever there was an excuse to make rank, being a "Tunnel Rat" was at the top.

EIGHTEEN

ANOTHER MEDAL PRESENTATION

It's amazing! Another Medal Presentation. We have them almost monthly. What for? I assure you we don't know. We were gathered in our Class A uniforms which, by the way we hate, to have a medal ceremony. My guys are always doing something heroic. I make out the paperwork and send it over to headquarters. We then go on about our business. I often wonder who reads these things. Here's what happens.

We gather and then we stand at attention while our names are read aloud. The medals are handed out to the individuals, and they thank whoever is the appointed hack of the day. The medal is then returned to the same hack who returns it to its case. Sometimes the medal count is long, sometimes the medal count is short. Most of the time the medal is from some action we have long forgotten. We may seem blasé, that the medals are a waste of time, as if we really don't care. Let me put it this way, we don't.

We never see those medals again. They go into the Central Intelligence Agency (CIA's) files and cease to exist. Just like us. Our medal count consists of Eight Silver Stars, 16 Bronze Stars, 18 Purple Hearts and, last but not least, Good Conduct medals for everyone. None of which we have. All reside in our files back in the bowels of the company we work for. Now, that being said, we don't work for medals. Our country seemed to think that in some small way we were contributing to the overall goal of victory.

The last time we were presented with some medals, we were attacked by rocket fire. There we all stood like idiots in Class A uniforms. We grabbed our rifles, which are always nearby and ran into the bush. We stopped at the edge of the jungle and took stock of ourselves and the situation. We were not about to run like fools into an ambush. We got organized. We all turned into scouts trying to find out where the enemy had stood or laid while they observed us. My men on our far right signaled to me that they were on the track. We moved toward them and proceeded into the jungle. My scouts were out in front of us leading the way. We knew by the way they recklessly left their trail that we were after ordinary people not soldiers. These people are recruited by the Viet Cong to find information that they could use against us. These same people were leading us to the Viet Cong.

We did not have our bows this time, just our trusty CAR-15's. The scouts sent back information as to the number and type of soldiers we were about to encounter. They were more than ordinary Viet Cong soldiers. These were rocket troops. More in number than we anticipated and better trained. We pulled in close and began to make a plan. One thing about us is that, we never back down. We decided that we would take them apart piece by piece. Rocket troops first as they were more organized. Viet Cong second, because they were village recruits and would probably run. We patiently waited until sunset. As they began to eat their evening meal, we began our approach. Silently and swiftly, we moved between the rocket launchers and began to fire our weapons as we emerged. The fight did not last long. In fact, it wasn't much of a fight.

We fired in one direction, they made a mad scramble toward their weapons and did not know which way to shoot. Later, we blew up all of their equipment. No combatant was left standing. We left nothing behind as usual. No one would know who was responsible for this carnage. We faded back into the jungle and covered the trail that both sides had used.

Now I had to make out more paperwork. Maybe we'll get some more medals.

NINETEEN

A LITTLE FALL NEVER HURT ANYONE

Patrol Boat, Riverine (PBR). That's a mouthful in any language. I had met Lt. Oscar at a seminar we had attended about how to investigate Vietnamese boats on rivers and Delta waters. Cross training. That is what it was called. HURONS on Boats? Sure, HURONS used small boats, they were called canoes. What genius dreamed this up?

Once again, I found myself doing something I had absolutely no training for. I was sent to cross train on river boats. None of my men were with me. I was on my own running hell bent for leather on a PBR captained by a cox'n, who was a genuine kamikaze pilot. These guys were loose cannons. They would run as fast as the boat would go and shoot up every square inch of the riverbank. Mainly they used the .50 caliber (cal.) machine gun that was perched on the bow. This was the life I envisioned for myself back when the Navy wouldn't have me. What a rush!

After a few days of river patrolling, I transferred to a Swift Boat unit. Instead of 32-foot fiberglass boats; these were made of aluminum and around 50-feet long with twin .50 cal. machine guns forward. These boats patrolled rivers and even out into the Gulf of Tonkin. This is where I met my Waterloo. Waterloo is where Napoleon met his largest defeat. As such meeting your Waterloo is bad, very bad.

The Gulf of Tonkin is large, very large with lots of commerce. River boats, Ocean boats, Sailing boats large and small. The captain spotted a small Chinese Junk, these boats have been around for a thousand years. Junks and Sampans were everywhere. Sampans for river transport, Junks were for deeper water. We approached the Junk which was about 35-feet long, turned on the siren for a few seconds and pulled alongside. Everything went by the numbers. The Junk owners, a Vietnamese family, produced their papers showing what cargo they were carrying, and we began our inspection. I opened a hatch that led into the interior of the boat. Looking down I could see the ladder that was used to enter the boat. I stepped onto the ladder and immediately fell toward the floor followed by the unsecured ladder. My fall was stopped by my boot. I was now hanging upside down by the sole of my boot. I was wearing my trusty Corcoran Paratrooper Boots. The sole of these boots extends almost a half-inch around the boot. There I was twisting back and forth like a salami hanging from a hook. The sole of my boot was wedged into the coming that the hatch cover rests on. My knee was taking the brunt of this insult to my body. The crew freed my boot and I collapsed into the interior of the Junk. After the inspection, the guys lifted me up and out and onto our boat. I wish I had a movie camera taking a movie of all this to show my men. I know they would see the humor in all of this.

My cross training came to an end with me on crutches. I was back on duty in a few days. As we all know when you are 25 you are bullet proof. The HURONS were bored with my stories and refused to listen to me after my first day back at base. I am really looking forward to our next assignment. Whatever it is it will be better than climbing in and out of Chinese Junks.

The knee didn't bother me for over 50 years. Now that I'm a little past my prime it doesn't always want to go the same way the rest of me wants to go.

TWENTY

CAN A JUNK BE JUNK?

There I was wandering the Harbor of Saigon. I was wearing civilian clothes seemingly just minding my own business. I was looking for a unique way for my men and I to make our way to North Vietnam. I wanted to blend in with the natives. I did not want to stand out while we sailed our way to Haiphong Harbor in North Vietnam. My reasoning was, buy an old boat and rebuilt it to our own specifications. In reality my own unique way to get in close to the shore and look like we belonged there.

I wandered along looking for something special. Then I saw it, half sunk into the mud. An old used up 50-foot-long Chinese Junk, well past it's prime. My vision seemed to be right there in front of my eyes. I wandered over to the Harbor Masters office and inquired if that half-sunk piece of garbage was for sale. That is when I learned that that pile of garbage was really the most valuable yacht in all of Vietnam. It wasn't half sunk it was, in reality, just soaking so that the timbers would swell up and fit together to keep the water out. The two missing masts were not missing but merely being used by another Junk that was due to return anytime. The hole in its side was there to let the water, which was used to swell the interior timbers, out. This ingenious idea worked because the rising tide filled the boat with water and the falling tide let the water out. I never would have thought of that idea and told the

Harbor Master it truly was a brilliant idea. He then told me that I could have the boat for 30,000 South Vietnamese Dong. I offered him 50 Dong and told him his work crews could do the work rebuilding the Yacht. He should have been an actor. His performance deserved an Academy Award. He informed me that I was taking the food out of his children's mouths. They would have to go to the school dressed in rags. Even bare footed. I loved his performance, so I offered another five Dong which he took and sold the boat to me. There were smiles all around. I made sure all of the serial numbers matched and had his assistant co-sign.

The boat was hauled out of the mud and washed to clear out any local organisms that were growing or swimming inside. The older Chinese Junks were built with the most beautiful Teak wood and would last over 100 years if taken care of. Teak is now considered an endangered species and can only be cut using special permits. We had the boat put inside a covered enclosure. Now the rebuilding could begin. The interior of a cargo Junk was enormous. We stripped out the living quarters leaving just the antique stove, we would need to cook on our trip. We built two man benches the inside length of the hull. Holes were bored thru the hull to match the height of the benches. The benches and holes were on both sides of the hull. We had the repair yard manufacture 20 extra-long oars that would pass through the holes. We would be rowing close to shore. The engine was replaced with a marine engine that was repurposed from a Navy shore boat. This engine was a lot more powerful than the puny original engine of the Junk. Of course, we needed a larger fuel tank to feed our new beast. It's amazing what a carton of American cigarettes will buy. We used several cartons during the rebuild. It was about this time of the rebuild that I had the bottom of the boat flattened. Sounds strange but the Junk had a deep round hull. We needed to get in close to shore and so we needed a flatter bottom along with a shorter rudder.

While the rebuild was taking place I had my men rent large rowing boats and practice rowing around the Harbor. The word was that they were getting ready for a rowing contest that was coming up in three months. At last, the Junk was ready. The final touch I gave it was a large Dragon painted on the bow along with round plugs that fit the round holes in the hull. It was time to go.

We loaded 100 of pounds of food and ammunition into the hidden compartments deep inside of the hull of our junk. Our CAR-15's were hidden the length of the deck along with spare magazines. It was then that I told my men that our real cargo was South Vietnamese Commando's. We would insert them along the coast of North Vietnam. One very dark night we heard running boots coming alongside of our boat. Commandos! We began loading the men onto our boat and showing them the way down inside of the Junk. We helped them stow their gear. At dawn I returned topside with three of my men and we prepared to cast off. With our engine running slow, we exited the Harbor turned the Bow north and began our journey. We observed radio silence and ignored all calls wanting to know who we were and where we were headed. I increased the engine rpm and we picked up speed. Our sails were strapped to their masts for use when we were in among the boats we would meet along our route. We figured it would take two days running under power. Sails by day power by night. The more we could use our engine the shorter the run time would be.

We had been running 24 hours when we spotted a sail on the horizon. Raising the main sail, we continued north. From a distance we looked like any Junk. Our speed was increased to compensate for the drag of the sail. We kept as much distance from the other boats as possible. We ran another 12 hours on our main course then made a turn toward the mainland and lowered our sail. As evening diminished our distance vision, we turned on the red lights inside the control room. Red lights allowed us to still see our gauges and not lose our night vision.

We had not seen any navigation lights from any vessels close by, so we continued to run with the navigation lights off. We turned off our interior red lights and just used the red-light feature of our flashlights. We were able to get a fix on our position from the radio and closed our distance to the shoreline. Our engine was noisy, so we ran out the oars and began to row toward the shore. Water was calm with the moon just a crescent in the sky. We inflated a rubber boat and set it into the water. Five Commandos loaded their gear into the boat then swimming alongside of their boat swam toward shore. We waited for a light signal that everything was OK, and we backed away and proceeded north. We repeated delivering the men to the shore four more times. After the last of the Commandos were safely ashore, we headed back out toward open water. We had been running about an hour when I ordered the running lights turned on. We headed south. Our Chinese Junk was a fabulous delivery vessel. I looked forward to turning it back into Yacht condition.

My lookout who was perched toward the top of the mainmast yelled down that he thought he had seen a shadow astern of us. We began to get ready for hostile action. The men erected the steel faced shields we had positioned around the boat and prepared to fight. We had several water bags around the deck. This was a wood boat so it would burn easily. We no longer looked like a Chinese Junk we looked like a fort. I had brought along several M-72 LAW (Light Anti-Tank Weapon) rocket launchers. These are very light and Tank killers; they would make short work of any small vessel we encountered. We were ready to fight and would not wait to exchange pleasantries. If the vessel was North Vietnamese, we would shoot first. The Vessel closed on our Starboard side. It turned a very bright searchlight on us which also illuminated its bridge showing us it's North Vietnamese emblem and flag. We fired the anti-tank rounds first. Three high-explosive rockets arched across our wake and exploded against the side of the vessels bridge. We followed with sub-machine gun fire from the CAR-15s. It was over in under a minute. A fourth rocket was fired next to the vessels waterline which put a very large hole into the boat, and it began to sink. We pulled away and ran our engine as fast as it would go for several hours then slowed down to conserve our fuel.

We were very low on fuel as we entered the harbor. All of the evidence of making war was safely stowed below deck. We looked like all of the other Junks in the harbor. I had three of my men on deck to handle the lines and secure us to the dock. We walked up to the Harbor Masters office to exchange pleasantries. We answered his questions as to how well the boat handled and if we enjoyed our voyage. We told him we had never been so pleased with a boat that handled as well as the one he had helped rebuild.

I asked him to make up some plans to turn it back into a Yacht. I explained that I would be back later that night to remove some equipment that I had found to be of no use to me. The rest of the men just kicked back inside of the Junk and waited for night to fall.

I had held many ranks during my service in Vietnam, but this was the first time I had been the captain of a boat.

TWENTY ONE

MY FAVORITE WRISTWATCH

We were going through my old photo albums a few weeks ago. While looking at one photo, mention was made about the wristwatch I had on. Obviously, one would not wear a watch that was as bright as that was. You could see its magnificence from a mile away. But it did have a place in the war, it was not just a timepiece. It was what was called a repeater. It would chime and tell time in two different hemispheres. In other words, you would not want to get it dirty. But it did have its place in the war.

There was a period in the war that I had to pretend to be what I was not. I was called upon to go up and down in rank several times. When dealing with village elders one could not be anything but a person of authority. I must pause and explain that I enjoyed every minute of my charade. The powers that be would not place themselves in a dangerous position, but were very happy to put me there. After all, what loss can a mere 2nd Lieutenant matter? I must say that I really looked good as a full Colonel. What lies these mortals tell.

Once upon a time I was tasked to put on my Colonel's regalia and take care of some trouble high up in the hills dealing with child brides. Messing around with long held traditions can get you killed. I had four of my men dress up in full HURON complete with war paint, looking fierce.

I wanted the elders to understand that I meant what I said.

We boarded the helicopter and flew off into the morning fog. I had never been to this location and hadn't met with anyone from this district. I was going to have to wing it. Should be a piece of cake. After all B.S. is my middle name. We flew for over an hour climbing most of the time. The helicopter was protesting when, finally, there they were. Two villages separated by a small hill. People were milling around waiting for the great peace maker. We circled around twice and then landed in a cloud of dust. Two of my men stepped out which made the people back up and then I got out wearing my mirrored sunglasses followed by my other two bodyguards. The sunglasses were used whenever I did not want anyone to see my eyes. I stepped forward and slightly bowed to the elders. My men crowded together with the elders. I had explained what I wanted them to do while we were in transit. I wanted them to look down on the elders for intimidation. These large men looking down on them would cause the elders to be nervous. Maybe even ready to make a deal.

We were ushered into a large hut that had been erected for our, as the HURONS would say, "Pow Wow" There I sat, listening to each tribe's complaint. These people traded young girls between the tribes. One tribe complained that the quality of young girls was not up to their standards. That the other tribe was sending girls as young as 11. The usual age was 13. I can't tell you what my thoughts were as to what was going on. At that time my wristwatch began to chime. What a fortuitous moment. Everyone in the hut focused on the sound coming from my wrist. A loud murmur arose from the elders sitting in the hut. The ruling elders were afraid. They thought demons were stirring and they became afraid. I told them that the gods were angry and were speaking to me from the wristwatch. The gods wanted the practice of marrying young girls to older members of the tribe to stop. Today! The elders were very unhappy but did not want to anger the gods. Making the gods mad was dangerous.

Now I had to seal the deal. I decided to use the watch as an omen. I explained that I would leave the watch in the temple that overlooked both villages. I had them send a teenaged boy to me in the temple. It was there I explained what could happen if the watch began to chime anytime instead of the noon hour. I explained that only the young boy was to wind the watch every day after it chimed the noon hour. I told the boy how to properly wind the watch. The elders were afraid and stood back. I made a rule that only after the girls began to menstruate plus one year could they be considered for brides. I wasn't happy with this arrangement, but I did not want to push too far. The elders weren't happy, but they were more afraid of what would happen if the watch became angry.

That watch should last many years as long as it is treated with care. I also told them that if I had to return it would make the watch very unhappy. I think that the last little warning worked wonders.

I radioed for our helicopter to return. I had the HURONS put on a show. They danced about and shot fire arrows into images of the villagers. I know it was hokey, but a little fear can go a long way. As for me, I was out one fine timepiece. If it helps the little girls enjoy their childhood, it was worth the cost.

TWENTY TWO

PEACE AT LAST

We found those words to be strangely ominous. Peace talks were to take place in the capital city of Cambodia. Phnom Penh a beautiful city thousands of years old. A peaceful and serene city of peace and neutrality. North Vietnam, South Vietnam along with the United States were to meet and discuss terms to stop the fighting and perhaps reunite the country.

It was a wonderful idea that every serviceman would agree to. I know I was in favor of it. Word had come down from Army Command to stop all field operations. We were to disengage from whatever we were doing and, at least in our case, pretend to let bygones be bygones. Pat everyone on the back and invite them over for tea. Here's the problem. We had stalked a large force of North Vietnam soldiers that were headed toward the south, for two weeks. They were moving-slowly through the jungle. Every night they would stop and make camp. Every night they would have guards patrol the perimeter of the camp. They did this to protect those who were within the perimeter of the camp. Every night my men would remove the guards and make them disappear.

I wish I could have filmed the commotion that occurred every morning when the officers could not find the guards. The soldiers searched the camp and even ventured a short way into the jungle and found nothing. The lost men were considered deserters. The officers berated their men and threatened them with death. They even doubled the guard. This meant that instead of one man there would be two at each sentry point. Twenty men would guard the camp instead of ten. We all thought that was great because getting rid of 20 men would really thin out the herd, so to speak.

We thinned and then pruned. The officers received dispatches, from a very primitive system consisting of two men on bicycles. This new information excited them, and they called the men together and explained that they were to double their efforts to cross the border to South Vietnam. That new information interested me also. I thought that it was time to extract the North Vietnam Army (NVA) officers and bring them along with their dispatches to our Headquarters.

Our plan was simple. We would wait until the camp had settled down and posted guards. At the stroke of 0100 hrs. We would eliminate half of the guards leaving the entire southern half of the camp unguarded. We then just walked into the camp, entered the Officers tent and proceeded to cover their mouths and noses with rags soaked in either. Making sure they were out we tied them up slung them over our shoulders and just walked them and the dispatches out of camp.

We rotated carrying the prisoners every one quarter of a mile until we reached just about four clicks, miles, away from camp. It was there we radioed our helicopter extraction group, using prearranged codes, to come and get us. We were just outside of the jungle on the South Vietnamese side of the border. I posted guards and we relaxed. We really had worked hard to retrieve the dispatches and

NVA Officers. I was really proud of my men. I felt we had hit a home run with the bases loaded.

I don't know why but I began to feel apprehensive. I could feel the hair begin to stand up on the back of my neck. My men had noticed it also. Maybe it was the vibration we all felt. We backed into the tree line of the jungle and watched and waited. A little over 200-feet off to our left side lumbered six NVA tanks. They appeared from the tree line side by side. They looked like a wall of steel. Hundreds of soldiers walked along with them. I sent my scouts into the jungle to find their edge, I did not want them to walk into us. I radioed the helicopters to hold back and send Fighter Bombers. I gave the coordinates and said I would back into the jungle at least two clicks, miles, and wait for them to tell me when all was clear. I began to wonder what was in those dispatches.

We retreated back into the jungle for about an hour when I called a halt. The men spread out to secure the area. We felt safe and began to hear loud explosions and cannon fire from the aircraft. It seemed that they were putting holes into any and everything that moved. At least we hoped that was what was happening. We waited over an hour and then the radio began to tell us of an all clear. We waited another half of an hour and began to move, once again, to the edge of the jungle. My men had spread out to make sure we didn't run into any objects who moved on two legs. I called the helicopters.

We stepped from the tree line and observed the utter devastation of the enemy. The power of the United States military became evident. I don't understand how anyone could stand up to that power and continue to fight. Much to my surprise our helicopters were hovering overhead.

I stayed off of the radio and signaled for them to land. We loaded our prisoners onto a helicopter along with a few of our men and then loaded the rest of us aboard another helicopter and lifted off into the wild blue yonder. The helicopter radio began to chatter something about a ceasefire. Everyone was to stand down. I told the Pilot it was too bad about the static coming through the speaker. We could not understand what was being said. After all we had been through, those prisoners were going to headquarters along with those dispatches. What they did with them was their responsibility.

We delivered our contribution to the war effort and had to endure a chastising fit for a group who had done everything asked of it. We were responsible for anything that went wrong with the peace talks. Never mind the invasion we had prevented. The dispatches did discuss pre-invasion plans but if there is a cease fire in place the fact that the NVA moved its army into the south won't be mentioned.

As I said earlier, the peace talks were to take place in Cambodia. The soldiers of HU-R-ON would be part of the Guard of Honor during the talks. We would wear the uniform of the United States Army. No weapons were allowed. This made sense as the talks were about peace. Both of the squads were to be present. We flew into Cambodia on a civilian aircraft. As we flew over Phnom Penh, we noticed a large company of armed guards surrounding the building where the negotiations were to take place. An uncomfortable feeling was overtaking us. Our instincts were beginning to make us uncomfortable. Why all of the firepower? We opened our duffle bags and brought out our Indian knives. These knifes were made with Obsidian blades, volcanic glass, with animal bone for handles. No metal for the detectors to pick up. These knifes were strapped to the backs of our men inside of their shirts. Each man would use the knife taken from the back of the man in front of him. Sixteen Hurons along with two Lieutenants and two radio operators deplaned. We were escorted toward a building in back of the Negotiating building. We began to smell a rat. As we approached the building, we began to pull out the shirt of the man in front of us. Reaching toward the knifes we began to bunch up. We turned to face the guards beside of us and saw they had placed magazines into their rifles. We instantly attacked. We used our knifes and became new owners of AK-47's. We turned and ran back to the Negotiation building. Upon entering we discovered that the Peace Committee had been taken prisoners.

As soldiers of HU-R-ON my men only know attack. We don't negotiate and as a rule don't take prisoners. We attacked every soldier in the building and for once took prisoners. These were high ranking politicians. We were counting on them to get us out. A little questioning by my Hurons gave us the real story. This farce wasn't about peace talks. Oh no, it was about the Huron soldiers. The whole of North Vietnam was terrified of them. They were desperate to rid themselves of those terrifying Native American soldiers. 'This was orchestrated by Hanoi.

Officials in Hanoi were terrified that they were going to be next. Kidnapped while they slept and transported to the South. They had planned to bomb the entire area where the negotiations were taking place. The only reason that they didn't was it would look bad if real negotiations were to take place. Cooler heads prevailed and we took off with hostages, just in case.

As I have always said, I am so proud to have served with those brave soldiers of HU-R-ON. They saved my life several times. The graduates of the Officer Candidate Schools are taught to lead from the front. The Patch on their shoulder reads "Follow Me"! That is the reason so many sad telegrams were sent to their families during the Vietnam War.

TWENTY THREE

FLYING OVER A JUNGLE

Have you ever flown over a heavily canopied jungle? Have you ever experienced a sea of green? How about miles and miles of not knowing where you were? Flying along, doors wide open, the wind trying to extract your helmet from your head? Sitting with your legs hanging out just inches from the landing skids, holding on tightly to your trusty weapon? Flying along with a few of your best friends knowing that wherever you land there will be death and destruction? Did you ever know that a few words shouted above the noise of gunfire and the whirling rotor blades of the helicopters might send your men to their deaths?

Forty-five years. Forty-five long years, and I still hear the sound of helicopters in my dreams. Forty-five years and I still wake up soaked in sweat. My heart pounding as I still give commands. I automatically lift my pillow and check for my .45. The same .45 that rode in a holster strapped to my side many years ago. The same .45 that I used to shoot Viet Cong fighters who were trying to kill my men. The power of that weapon still brings a sense of unequaled power to this day. Hopefully, someday I'll be able to place my trusty friend in my gun safe and sleep in peace. Maybe someday I'll be able to heed the words of the medical officers to 'stand down'. The officers tell me that it is okay to 'stand down'. I reply to them that I have not received any communication that will tell me to quit all operations. Maybe it's because my group never existed. Maybe it's because there is no one left in the Pentagon or CIA, who have any idea of what we were doing. Maybe it's because there is no one to write that cease-and-desist letter.

No one left? Well, there are still a few of us who know too much. Even I, who knows the most, will not speak of the truth. Even now, I will only write the bare facts of the operations. I dance around the fires writing of the stories that are fit to print for public consumption. My stories are a salute to the brave soldiers who served our country. They deserve the public's adulation far more that I. Even now I expect a knock at my door. Maybe, someday I'll get that order to "stand down" and will be able to place my .45 in the gun safe and sleep in peace.

TWENTY FOUR

STARING DEATH IN THE FACE AGAIN

I received a large package in the mail last week from one of my men who stayed in 'Nam' when I rotated home. The note with it explained what was inside. He was leading a patrol into the jungle along the same trail where I had led them. The same trail where I had almost fought my last battle. His point man halted the patrol and sent back for him to come forward. There in the middle of the trail lay a large decomposing head of a snake. It looked vaguely familiar. As he studied it one eye opened, stared at him and closed. He noted a very small tail beginning to grow from the base of the head. He immediately scooped it into an empty gas mask bag. He then called a halt to the patrol and returned to basecamp. Back at 'camp' he put it into a refrigerated box and left it there.

After he rotated home, he never told his wife what was inside of the box. All he told her was that if anything happened to him, she was to send the box along with the sealed note addressed to me. She wrote that she had gone to work one day leaving him with the box as he wanted to look at it. When she returned from work, she found him lying on the floor with his face heavily cut and bleeding. He was moaning something about a snake and to get the box to me. He was unconscious when the ambulance crew delivered him to the hospital. He was still in the hospital when she finally shipped the box to me.

What could be in a box that was so dangerous? Certainly nothing could still be alive. I studied that box. I listened to that box. Not a sound. I shook the box. Nothing. Sure, the box was heavy, but what could be inside that had left a healthy man so critically injured. Maybe what attacked him wasn't even in the box.

I placed the box two feet away from my bed and leaned back against the bed. Since I had herniated a disc in my back some years ago, I have needed some support when lifting heavy objects. So, there I was with one leg along each side of the box. Suddenly the phone rang, and I had to get up to answer it. A good buddy I have known since our time in the army was downstairs and wanted to come up and spend some time. I pushed the buzzer to open the door and waited. In a moment he was at the door and came inside. We talked about old times, and I told him about our friend who was in the hospital. I mentioned the box, now residing near my bed, and that I was just about to open it.

There we stood starring down at the box. With two steps he was alongside of the box and opened it. Out sprang the head followed by a tail some two feet long. Spitting and hissing it hit my friend square in the face. Its fangs were slicing down his cheek as it fell to the floor. I made a dive for my Tomahawk, which has laid next to my bed for years. As I tried to strike at the head, that tail was whipping and tripped me. Down I went, landing next to the head. My back was wrenched, and I lay gasping staring into that face of death. I felt something pulling the Tomahawk from my grasp. I tried to hold onto it but was unable to thanks to my back which had gone into spasms.

Much to my surprise my buddy had taken that Tomahawk and was slicing into that head and cutting it into small pieces. I didn't think he would ever stop. What a mess. Sure, hope room service can clean up the mess.

It pays to have friends and a tomahawk.

ABOOKS

ALIVE Book Publishing and ALIVE Publishing Group
are imprints of Advanced Publishing LLC,
3200 A Danville Blvd., Suite 204, Alamo, California 94507

Telephone: 925.837.7303
alivebookpublishing.com

www.ingramcontent.com/pod-product-compliance
Lightning Source LLC
Chambersburg PA
CBHW030528260626
47157CB00005B/1935